My Secret CEO Santa

MAYA MOORE
ALINA MARTYN

Content Warnings & Tropes

Daddy Dom dynamic, Instalust/Obsession,
Grumpy x Sunshine, billionaire, Power
Imbalance, Short, No Cheating, HEA
Guaranteed

ONE
Julia

J ust $250. I just need to make another $250 and I'll be able to afford the ticket. I repeat over and over. I forced another fake smile on my face and adjusted the very annoying elf hat that had jingle bells on the end.

"I can do this." I sighed, slamming the locker door shut and awaiting Kyle's inevitable harassment.

Kyle was the general manager of Westin Mall and unfortunately, my immediate supervisor. He decided that he was going to be the manager of *The Christmas Spot* this year, a job that actually forced him to be away from the back office and make him work for his paycheck rather than just creepily watch people in the security cameras.

Every single fucking shift he decided to hit on me. His beer belly was barely contained by the stained short-sleeved button downs he wore, and he had a disgusting habit of wiping his sweaty hands repetitively on his shit-brown pants.

"Julia, Julia, Julia," Kyle said, resting his arm over his head on the door frame into *The Christmas Spot*. "You're here."

Ugh.

"I am. Just like every Tuesday, Wednesday, Thursday and Friday for the past month and a half." *Be nice, Julia. Be nice.* I needed this job to be able to make it home for Christmas.

I lived in and went to a private university that's about a twelve hour drive from my hometown. The full-ride scholarship I worked my ass off for in high school meant I didn't have to worry about tuition, food or books, but anything else was on me. My car was not working well enough to make the long drive, so that's out of the question. My parents are having their own financial troubles right now and made it very clear Christmas would be extremely lean this year, so I couldn't ask them for help.

"What a good little elf you are." Kyle tried to smile in a way that he might think was hot, but really just made him look constipated. He leaned closer. Hot cigarette breath wafted into my nostrils.

"If you just excuse me," I tried to slide past him, but his arm jut out and blocked my path. I sighed. *Every fucking day.* "Kyle."

"Oh hush now, Jules." He shushed me, and I clenched my fists. I fucking hated being shushed.

"Kyle!" The new guy entered the small hallways connecting the locker room and *The Christmas Spot.* He's tall, really tall. At least 6'5 and dressed from head-to-toe like Santa. The newcomer took one look at Kyle and I, and his eyes narrowed dangerously. His words were tense and clipped when he said, "Kyle, I think we're ready to open. If you're ready."

That voice. So dark and deep, smooth like honey. I wanted to hear him talk again.

"Thanks, Seth." Kyle barely spared a glance over his shoulder as he spoke, keeping his gaze locked on me. His words were meant to dismiss Santa, but he stayed. He stayed and never took his eyes off of me.

"You can go now." Kyle tried once again to dismiss Santa, looking over his shoulder and gestured towards the door.

"No, I can't actually," Seth said. He moved

his hands out of his pockets, and I got a glimpse of his massive fingers rolled into a fist that I knew would take Kyle out in one single punch. "I need her to open the line and start taking information. *That* is the job she is here for. Not to be harassed.." A dark eyebrow arched, and in that one move, was actively challenging Kyle.

All to protect me. And I had to fight the urge to get on my knees for him in thanks.

Staying silent, I watched the exchange, hoping that Kyle backed off. I didn't want to feel his hands on my skin again. And I really couldn't lose this job because I knocked my boss's two front teeth out. But this Seth guy didn't seem to have that same fear.

"Fine," Kyle snapped, hitting the wall right by my head in frustration and dropping his arm. "Until later, Julia." He said with a sneer and walked away, leaving me with my tall savior.

"Does he do that shit a lot?" Santa asked, even through the plastic-y bushy white beard his strong cheekbones poked through. "I swear, I never knew." He looked at me with such sincerity in his dark eyes that I stood there for an extra few moments just mesmerized.

"Sure, I mean how could you? We're just temps. I just have to make it through a few more weeks and then I'm out of here."

"Did he touch you?" Santa sneered, his hands ripped from his pockets and he pulled the red hat off. "I swear I'll kill that fucker." He growled, his eyes blazed with fury. I just shook my head no, too enthralled with how hot the energy he exuded. Powerful, strong, virile. *Sexy*.

He crumpled the red Santa hat in his hands, showing me the salt and peppered brown hair as he ran a hand through the loose waves. He was clearly much older than me and so, so hot. "I apologize."

"For what? You aren't a creep who can't keep his hands to himself." I chuckled and walked towards the overly decorated spare store.

"True." He set his hat back on his head. His eyes, the only part of *him* I could actually see, seemed sad. "But that doesn't mean that I'm still not sorry that it's happened to you. I won't let it happen again."

I smiled softly. What a sweet, naive man. What could he actually do?

"Whatever you say, Mr. Claus."

That earned me a smile of bright white teeth underneath the white plastic strands.

"Right this way, *Jules*," Santa said, his voice dropped even lower and deeper. The tone made me shiver as I walked past him into the room to see a line of excited kids bouncing on their toes and looking around the others in line to try and get a sneak peek at Santa Claus. "Let's go make some kids happy."

It was a constant repeat of; putting a kid on Sexy Seth's lap, giving them a candy cane, taking a photo and then thanking them for coming while pushing them out of the gate so I could get the next kid. Over and over for hours. I only got to talk to Seth in short spurts; "Do you need some water?" "Yes, thanks." "Can you sneak me a candy cane next time?" "Only if you're good."

That one got him a wink. I could feel his heavy gaze covering every inch of me every time I walked by him. It was really turning me on to be honest.

Three O'Clock rolled around quickly and for that I was thankful. *Break time.*

"Everyone, just your friendly helper elf

here." I spoke loudly enough for the room full of chattering adults and children to hear me. "I just wanted to let you all know that Santa has to go to his workshop for about 20 minutes. Thank you!" I waved to all the groaning patrons and grabbed Santa's hand, leading him to the backroom.

"Finally," I muttered.

"This was a lot more intense and emotionally significant than I thought it would be." Santa pulled his hat and wig off. My mouth dropped and he smirked confidently, but also a little cocky, at me.

"Hi, I'm Seth Alexander." He squeezed my hand, and I remembered that we were holding hands, probably for too long. I jerked my hands back awkwardly.

"I'm Julia." As the words left my mouth I wanted to cringe. "You knew that already." He smirked at me and chuckled. Not in a way that made me think he was laughing at me, but in a way that he might have thought was cute that he caused me to be flustered.

"I know," Seth said, sitting down and grabbing a drink of water. "Those kids," He sighed. "They're so cute. I almost feel guilty about lying to them."

"You're bringing them so much

happiness." I grabbed my own water and sat next to him. It was nice to sit in the quiet after the non-stop of the Christmas music over the speakers, the chatter of the parents, the buzz of the kids, all mixed with anticipation, joy, and frustration. "I'm sure your arms are tired though." I fought the urge to grab his arm and massage it, my eye having caught the muscles barely being contained within the red material. I tried my best to keep from staring when he would lift each kid to set them on his lap.

My thighs clenched as a fantasy of being lifted by his big arms and set on his lap, but not in an innocent, sweet way, invaded my brain. I'd straddle him and ride him on his chair, asking Daddy Claus if I was naughty or nice while he would growl in my ear how good I was for him.

"No, it's not bad." He waved me off and I literally had to shake my head to clear the fantasy.

Fuck, now I'm turned on.

"What do you do when you're not dressed as a little elf?" He asked.

"I'm in my junior year of college."

"Studying what?"

"Business. How about you?"

He bit his lip with a grin like he was hiding a secret. "The most important thing I'm doing right now is helping these kids believe in the magic of Santa. And hanging out with *my* little elf, of course." Seth winked at me and took a drink of water.

Fuck me, Daddy.

The thought made me jump with shock, but turned me on more than I ever thought a word could. I gulped and felt my heart race at his words. At being called *his*.

"We only have a few minutes left before we're thrown back into the fray. Do you need anything?" He asked me gruffly. So nicely taking care of me. *Just you, Daddy.*

"I just have to run to the bathroom. I'll be right back." I had to go cool myself off because this tension between us was going to ruin my panties soon.

"I'll be waiting."

"I bet you will, Mr. Claus." I smirked, and gave him a wink of my own.

TWO

Seth

Sassy little elf. I'd like to turn her over my knee and spank the naughty out of her. Then she could call me Santa all she wanted.

I watched her sweet ass sway as she strode down the hallway. She'd run away. Trying to avoid the overwhelming attraction sparking between us. The corner of my mouth twitched.

She disappeared around the corner. I had to follow her. There was no other choice. I trailed after the sweet little elf, reaching the hallway with a few long strides. When I was informed about the lack of staffing and the fucking flake of a Santa we'd hired, I'd had no choice but to fill the position. My secretary kept going on about it being good for publicity.

After seeing Julia, I didn't give one shit about the publicity. I just want her.

I turned another corner and strode through the door to reach the second hallway.

Ah, just as I thought. The little elf was slumped against the wall, with her head tilted back and her eyes closed. I approached her but she didn't open her eyes until I stood directly before her. Blue eyes stared up at me, sucker punching me in the gut. I wanted her. Badly. Her eyelashes fluttered slightly, desire clear in the expressive, beautiful pools.

With another step closer, I was flush against her. Her warm little body against me. Her eyes widened up at me. She could feel the thick length of my hard cock.

She shuddered, her body curving toward me.

"Naughty little elf," I said gruffly. I cupped her hip, bringing her against me and bending her back until I could lean down to press my lips to hers. I swept my tongue inside her mouth, pillaging and owning it with swift, demanding swipes. She was so pliable against me, so giving. She whimpered, and my cock twitched. "I want you, baby."

"Yes." Her soft voice affected me viscerally. I would ruin men for her. All men but me. I *was* going to ruin one for daring to make a move on her. "I want you, Seth."

My name on her lips caused precum to surface at my tip. I groaned. "You're making a mess of me, baby."

"I can clean it up." Her fingers slipped into the bright red costume's waistband.

"Fuck yes," I groaned. My cock throbbed. "But not here, no one gets to see you but me."

"Oh," she whispered, looking down the hall as if she had forgotten where we stood. Fuck. That innocent look disarmed me. I looped my arm around her waist and guided her down the white tiled hall, almost carrying her in my haste to one of the storage closets. The doorknob turned and I shuffled her inside. The soft yellow light above fell over her hair, emphasizing the pale colors woven through her hair. The door clicked shut.

"Clean me off, little elf."

She dropped to her knees without hesitation and the bells on her hat jingled.

Explosive lust ravaged my insides. Her small hands hooked under the waistband of my costume as well as my boxers, pulling them down in one motion. My cock sprang free, the mushroom tip glistening with cum.

She exhaled and the soft caress of her breath made my balls tighten.

"*Fffff*uck," I grunted. What was this maddening lust making it impossible for me to control myself? I studied her hovering over the tip of my cock, her brilliant blue eyes peeking up at me. Another rush of precum rose and leaked down the side of my cock. My naughty little elf was teasing me.

And I wouldn't take it anymore. I knocked the hat off her head and slipped my fingers into her silky hair, bunched it, and used it to guide her onto my cock. Her warm lips spread tightly around my head. She felt so fucking good.

A groan wrenched free from my throat. I forced her down another inch. She was pliable, allowing me to guide her. She was perfect.

I suppressed the urge to tilt my head back, wanting to see her take my cock in her soft, wet mouth.

"Relax your jaw, baby."

She did as I ordered, making my cock so hard it hurt. She took more of my length as her pouty pink lips stretched around me. Heat in my gut swelled. The throb became excruciating. She took hold of the base of my cock and with a suck, she glided her hand against the base of my shaft.

A wrenching release took hold, making all thoughts fade. All that formed was utter and absolute tingling pleasure. My cock throbbed again and again, feeding her. And she sucked every drop of me down.

I slammed my palm down on the shelf to my side to steady myself. She'd made my knees weak. I panted, shocked to my core.

This woman . . . was different.

I yanked my pants back up and cupped her waist to stand her up. She stumbled to the side, and I steadied her.

"You okay, baby?"

"Yeah, my legs fell asleep." The corner of her lips tipped up. "Look at that worry on your face. You give me such 'daddy' vibes."

Daddy? Oh fuck yes.

"Julia," I hissed. "Call me that again." Her eyes brightened with excitement.

"Yes, daddy."

I cupped her cheek and leaned down to press my mouth against hers. Tasting myself on her tongue.

"Now, it's my turn to please you," I murmured.

A beep assaulted the small room, making her jump.

"Break is over." She scooped her phone out of her pocket and shut the ringing off.

"A little longer." I couldn't let her go.

"I can't risk getting fired." Anxiety played over her features and I bit back my demand for more.

"I'll see you out there." I finally settled on. She smiled, relieved.

I patted her ass as she swayed past me and shut the door. Taking a deep breath, I fished into my pocket and pulled my cell phone out to call my secretary.

"Mr. Westin?"

"Don't submit those images to the marketing department." I snapped, receiving only silence from the other end. "And fire Kyle down in the events department."

"May I ask the reason, Mr. Westin?"

Pissing me off.

"Harassment."

THREE

Julia

T he next morning, for the first time, I was actually excited to get to work. I wasn't overwhelmed with dread about having to put on a fake smile all day.

I knew that today, my smile would be genuine.

Seth was... Well, he was something else.

That kiss was the best kiss of my life, and his dominance... wow. Not to mention the *'Daddy'* that had slipped out... I'd never been so turned on.

As I stuffed my bag into my locker, I grabbed the red-and-green striped elf hat to complete my over-the-top festive ensemble. Just as I went to close the locker door, two big arms wrapped around me, and a warm, hard body pressed tightly against my back.

I knew instantly who it was by the heavy pine and sandalwood scent, and relaxed into the embrace.

"Jules," Seth whispered in my ear. "Good morning, I missed you last night."

"Daddy," I whispered with a small whine, holding onto his forearm. "I could barely sleep after yesterday. My panties were ruined."

"Good." Seth groaned, and stepped back, spinning me in his arms so our foreheads touched. "Have you been good for Daddy, little elf?" Daddy growled in my ear.

"Yes." One of his hands slid down my waist slowly before he dipped it lower and reached for the hem of my short red skirt. Was he going to take me here? Did I want that?

Who was I trying to fool? Of fucking course I wanted that. I wanted everything he was willing to give me.

I wanted more of this.

I wanted everything.

"What do you want for Christmas, baby? Have you been good?" His words lingered in my ear, as I was too lost in the sensation and anticipation of what was happening to really focus. Seth's other hand went up, slipping under the back of my shirt and his warm, rough touch tickled my skin.

"Snow," I blurted, and froze in his arms. Worried that he'd think I was weird. But it was the truth. I was missing the white Christmas I always had back home in Michigan and might not have here.

Luckily, Seth didn't miss a beat. His hands kept roaming my body, bringing me goosebumps, and causing my panties to dampen.

"Snow, you say?" He nosed his way down the column of my neck and bit down lightly on my pulse point.

"Yes," I moaned. "Snow. Enough to make a snow angel and cover everything. Just like back home in Michigan."

"Daddy Santa will see what he can do, baby."

I let the conversation drop because I didn't actually expect him to be able to deliver my want of snow, but it was just nice to be able to think of the nostalgic need for the kind of Christmas that I've always enjoyed.

"It's almost time for us to get out there." Panting, I let my head drop back against the wall as Seth's hands started sliding the hem of my skirt higher than was decent.

"Be a good girl for me. I'll take care of you."

"Yes, Daddy." His fingers were so long that when he cupped my ass, his fingertips nearly touched my pussy. I knew that if he moved even just slightly, he would've been able to feel how wet I was for him already.

"I guess we shouldn't keep them waiting, Julia." He kissed along my jaw before stepping back and leaving me cold where his warmth had just been pressed against my body.

A wolfish smirk covered his face as he slipped the Santa beard on quickly, pulled the red hat on his head, and walked out of the break room door. Leaving me in my mess of horniness.

Fucking tease.

Break time came around, and to my frustration, Daddy spent most of it talking with someone on his phone. He paced back and forth across the break room, so I was tasked with going to get us coffee.

He was lucky he's cute.

I handed him his *disgusting* black americano and walked off, annoyed that I didn't get the attention I wanted at break. I had been hoping that he would finish what he had started earlier.

"Hey, baby." Daddy grabbed my arm, pulling me into him. "Can you stay after work?"

I shrugged."Sure." My tone was clipped, but he ignored it and smiled.

"Good." I could see the happiness I'd brought to him. The little bit of darkness in his eyes had lifted temporarily. Seth lifted the beard to hook the white plastic over his face to become Santa again, but I stopped him. He paused with a confused look, and I surged up to capture the hard, needy kiss I wanted.

Wrapping my arms around his neck, he wrapped both of his around my waist and lifted me up. I fought every urge to hold myself around his hips and grind down to get the friction I really fucking needed.

"Santa's coming!" We froze with a jolt when we heard the squeal of a small kid from the other room, effectively breaking our bubble and bringing us back to Earth.

"After." He promised.

"After."

After every last kid took their picture with Santa, sat on his lap, and requested what they wanted placed under their tree on Christmas morning, it was finally quitting time.

Seth took a wad of keys out of his pocket and locked the front door with a sigh. With a wink to me, he pulled down each of the blinds to officially close *The Christmas Spot* for the evening.

"What did you want to see me for?" I asked with a coy smile, putting my hands behind my back.

"Come with me." Seth took my hand and walked me through the break room and into the other vacant storefront that was connected to the breakroom. This one was rented out as needed, but was currently empty.

"Daddy?" I asked, slightly worried and nervous in the dark.

"Just wait," He whispered to me in the darkness. His hand left mine for one moment and in the next, the room was bathed in light. It was so bright the gleaming seemed to reflect off of every surface.

Just like the morning after a fresh snowfall.

Snow covered everywhere I could see.

With my Daddy standing right in the

middle in his bright red Santa pants and a tight gray t-shirt showing off his impressive physique. He stood with his arms stretched out wide and a big smile on his face.

"How?" I asked, tears forming in the corners of my eyes.

"I pulled a few strings." He shrugged like the most thoughtful gift I had ever gotten was not a big deal. "Do you like it?"

Did I like it?

"I fucking love it." I ran and jumped, wrapping my legs around his waist and his strong arms caught me with ease. "Thank you,"

"You're welcome," he said, resting his forehead against mine. I kissed him sweetly, grinding myself against him with appreciation.

"I'm totally going to make a better snow angel than you." I taunted, jumping down to feel the powdery softness of the artificial snow. It might not have been as cold or melt like real snow did, but it was a great substitute.

"I'm sure you can, baby girl." He chuckled.

Sticking my tongue out at him, I laid down on the ground and started making my angel. Instead of getting on the ground with me, he stood above, watching me with a fond smile.

"Aren't you going to make one?" I asked.

"I want to watch you. You being happy might just be my new favorite thing." He pulled his phone out of his pocket and snapped a few pictures. I made sure to pose for them in every way. I'm sure I looked like a mess; my blonde hair fanned around my face, a too-big smile as I grinned up at him so hard my reddened cheeks hurt, my eyes shined with tears I hadn't let fall, and the ridiculous red and green elf costume I hadn't changed out of yet.

But I was *happy*. For the first time in a long time. And it was all because of Seth, because of my Daddy.

I didn't know how long we rolled around in the snow. It had to have been hours. My cheeks hurt from laughing and my heart was full. As I felt the night close, I realized I didn't want it to end. I didn't want to go back to my apartment alone and have to wait to see him the next morning.

I wanted more.

I wanted him.

"It's getting late, baby. What do you say

we-" I cut him off with a kiss. It was hard and fast, needy and desperate, but it showed him exactly what I wanted to do.

"Julia," He tried to pull back and ask me something, but I wasn't having it.

I was going to have this man, and I wanted him *now*.

"Where can we go?" I asked, taking delight in how bruised his plush lips looked.

Daddy didn't wait, didn't pause. He knew what he wanted too and stood up, pulling me up with him.

"Come with me." He grabbed my hand and pulled me into his side. Pushing the door open into the closed and deserted mall, we walked through the darkness that was only illuminated by exit signs and each store's emergency lights until he got to a utility door.

"Where are we?" I whispered.

"There are offices back here. I want to properly spread you out to enjoy you," he said huskily as I walked past him into the maze of hallways. Seth grabbed my hand and led me to an office at the end.

"Whose office is this?"

"The CEO," he answered.

The CEO? My eyebrows raised and I knew we were playing with fire.

"What if there are cameras?"

"I'll make sure that the footage is wiped. Don't worry." Daddy growled, grabbing my neck, and pulling me in for a searing kiss. I could feel his hard cock pressing against me and I shivered with anticipation at what was to come.

"Promise me, Daddy."

"I promise, little elf."

FOUR

Seth

Her delicious gingerbread and peppermint smell overwhelmed my senses. Comforting, delicious, and fucking maddening. I craved this woman like the next breath in my lungs.

I rubbed my thumb against the fluttering pulse at the base of her throat as I plunged my tongue into her mouth. She met the caress of my tongue with as much passion. Her soft little moan into my mouth made my cock jerk. Fuck. She was everything I wanted and hadn't known I needed.

I corralled her against the door, pressing myself into her lush body.

"Hang onto me naughty girl," I whispered huskily. Her arms snaked up and hooked around my neck. I hoisted her legs up and around my hips in a smooth motion.

Yes. Her sweet cunt lined up with my cock perfectly. I groaned. Holding her around her thighs, I propped her against the door and angled back so she could slide her small hands between us.

"Unbuckle me," I ordered. Her trembling hands fumbled with my zipper, but finally, my cock sprang free. The wet, aching tip bobbed, and her slim fingers wrapped around me. Electricity zinged down my shaft and drew my balls tight to the base. Just one touch and she had me so fucking close to erupting. Her thumb caressed my mushroom tip, eliciting more moisture.

"Do you like that, Daddy?"

"*Fuck*, you naughty little elf."

Growling, I delved under her green elf dress and ripped her tights off with a smooth jerk. The fabric tore away with ease, baring her. I wanted to eat out her sweet pussy, and I'd make sure there would be time later. My cock ached to be in her– now.

Her shoulders balanced against the wall and I tipped her hips up high, positioning her for me. I never fucked without a condom, but I didn't fucking care with her. I plunged deep inside, sliding in until my balls slapped her bare ass. Her pussy fluttered around my shaft, wringing a groan from my throat. I splayed her legs as wide as she could spread them. Withdrawing my hips, I slammed back in, making her shoulders thump against the wall. She gasped and bit her plump lower lip.

She drove me to fucking madness.

I slammed into her again and again, her little needy breaths escaped her despite how hard she tried to keep quiet.

Her channel gripped my cock and her hands around my neck tightened, her little fingernails pressing into my skin. When her pussy fluttered around my cock, I gritted my teeth, withholding my release. I was so fucking close, but I didn't want this to end.

I ceaselessly thrust even though her legs started to twitch desperately with every pump. Her cunt fluttered.

She was going to come again.

My orgasm gripped my balls and drew them tight. The sudden release ripped a groan from my throat. The sound was guttural, needy, and only for her. Gripping her waist tight, I slammed into her, chasing the violent swell of release. She. Was. Maddening. I withdrew my hips to slam back into her. My cock spasmed, releasing a jut of cum into her slick channel. Making her *mine*. My chest pumped up and down. Fuck, I'd never come so hard. She was magnificent. I pressed my forehead against her. Her blue eyes were half-lidded with satisfaction.

I kissed her, swiping my tongue against hers. Her heat clasped my cock. I lifted my head and words hovered on my tongue. The truth of who I was . . . but I couldn't help being worried. What if she became just like all the others, only wanting me for my money? I liked how she saw me as just Seth, just Daddy. I wanted to keep this feeling a little while longer.

A hollow knock pounded against the door and I clamped my hand over her mouth before she let out the scream I could tell bubbled to the surface. Her blue eyes widened over my hand. Such large, beautiful eyes—

I shook off the besotted thoughts.

"We're going to get fired," she choked out, fear clear in her eyes.

"Quiet," I murmured.

I scooped up her fallen heels and took hold of her arm. Dragging her into my closet where I stored my personal items for when I had to stay and work late, I lightly shoved her inside.

She stumbled and I tossed the heels on the ground so they were out of view. Shutting the door, I strode to the door as I fastened the red pants from my costume.

Rob, my brother, stood at the threshold with that perpetual smirk on his face.

What the fuck was he doing here? I gave him a job in the security department so he could keep out of my way.

"Uh, hey," he cleared his throat. He tried walking through the threshold, but I stepped in his way to block the path. "Man, is it true?" He lowered his voice. "That you're fucking Julia Richards?" I narrowed my eyes. My brother was nosy as fuck.

I knew where every single camera in this building was and I knew that we had not been anywhere near them. That meant that someone was starting rumors.

Fuck. Fuck. Fuck. This would cause unnecessary bullshit.

She couldn't find out who I was.

Not until I was ready to tell her and I wanted to be the one to explain the situation. I couldn't let my big mouth brother run his mouth and fuck this up for me.

"Julia? The mousy blonde playing elf to

your Santa?" Complete and utter bullshit. That woman was not mousy, she was fucking sexy.

"I have nothing to do with her. We're barely acquaintances." I said, lacking any inflection.

"Oh," he pursed his lips and furrowed his eyebrows in confusion.

I strode to my door, opened it and raised an eyebrow pointedly. The thunderous expression on my face likely clued him in to not fuck with me right now. Thankfully, he lowered his head as he hurried out.

I slammed the door and hurried to collect my woman from the closet. She shoved the door open before I even turned the knob and she hurried past me so quickly I couldn't see her face.

"Talk later," she called. I frowned at her hasty retreat.

There was no way she'd overheard our conversation. It wasn't possible. I'd secured the door. Right?

I turned my wrist to check the time. Our break was about to be over.

FIVE

Julia

W hat the fuck?

My heart sank as I heard him say those words from the crack in the door. Is that what he thought of us? He made it sound like I was a quick fuck and nothing more.

It had to be that, because if he felt differently, he'd have defended me and told him that we were seeing each other. Instead, he fucking *shrugged* and said that we were "barely acquaintances'. That hurt.

Well, fuck him.

I walked into the break room, intent on ignoring him until I could get him alone to wring his neck.

"Julia?" His eyes widened when he caught up to me. I was angry, embarrassed, and I did not want to see him. My eyes narrowed and I pursed my lips angrily. Seth took a hesitant step towards me.

Oh, no, no, no, no. That was not happening.

I stepped out of his reach and raised an eyebrow. "Seth." I said, and walked off.

Storming out of the breakroom, I checked my watch and saw that I had just enough time to be alone for a few moments to get my emotions under control. Deciding that I deserved a pretzel for dealing with all the bullshit, I left with a huff.

Under all my anger, what I was really feeling was embarrassed and used. Why are men such dicks? Such idiotic morons.

"Julia. Julia, wait." Seth came gliding toward me like a predator in a Santa suit. People just naturally got the fuck out of his way. It would be quite the sight to see if I wasn't so pissed off at him.

"I have nothing to say to you."

"Just listen," He tried to grab my arm to force me to look at him, but I wasn't having any of that. I ripped my arm out from his grip.

"No, I heard what you said. I get it. We're nothing. Barely acquaintances. But yet, you've come in my pussy. Bare. That seems like we're a little more than acquaintances, if you ask me." I narrowed my eyes at him, feeling the blush warm my cheeks, but refusing to shrink back.

"Naughty words, little elf." He raised an eyebrow in challenge. "Let's go somewhere private to talk and you can yell at me all you'd like."

Crossing my arms over my chest, I conceded. Only because I really wanted to give him a piece of my mind and make Seth see how he hurt me. I wasn't going to stand for being used and discarded.

"Come on, baby." He gently put my hand in the crook of his elbow and guided me back towards *The Christmas Spot*.

"How could you say that?" I asked, trying to keep the hurt out of my voice, but failing.

"Baby," Daddy pulled me to him, back into the warmth of his embrace. "I... I just don't feel the need to put our business out there. I was trying to protect you." He opened the door to the break room, ushering me back there with an open arm.

I scoffed.

"Protect me? By telling him that I'm basically nothing?"

His brown eyes flashed with anger. "You're *everything* to me. How dare you say that."

"That's pretty much what you said!" I stomped. Embarrassment made my cheeks blush bright red as I realized that I stomped my foot like a child.

Daddy smirked, leaning back and resting his shoulder against the wall while crossing his arms over his broad chest. He looked like a wolf about to pounce.

"Are you feeling like I've not given you enough attention?"

"I'm feeling like you feel as if you can fuck me, be my Daddy, but then not actually claim me." I turned so my back was to him.

The tension in the room felt thick and uncomfortable.

"I want to claim you. I want you to be *mine* completely. I just don't want those slimy, nasty fucks to try to use you to—" He stopped talking.

"To use me for what?"

"I don't want them to use you, period. I'll make it known that you're mine. I promise." Daddy's hands rested on my hips, twisting me around so that he could look at me. "I'm sorry."

I melt a little bit.

"Don't let it happen again."

"Never," he said. He leaned down to place a small, hesitant kiss on my collarbone.

"You'll need to make it up to me."

"I will. Daddy will take good care of you, baby." He pulled me into his arms, kissing me roughly. It only took a moment of hard kisses and a few strategic grinds for me to feel his length harden again under the Santa suit.

"Then prove it." I bit my lower lip and watched as his eyes dropped to my lips.

"Naughty little elf." He growled, slipping his hands under my ass and roughly wrenching me up into his arms.

"Fuck me again, Daddy." I whispered in his ear.

"Gladly." Daddy looked around us, and I buried my face in his neck, kissing and sucking to mark him as mine.

"I can't make it to m-the office this time." He groaned, talking more to himself than to me. "Closet it is." He decided, moving us to the only room in the break room area that had a lock. The utility closet.

The memory of before made my pussy clench.

"You're going to have to be quiet, okay

baby? Can't have anyone walk in on us." Daddy muttered in my ear.

I nodded into his neck, biting down and gave his pulse point a hard suck. Surely that'll leave a mark.

He opened the door and pushed me inside, locking the door behind us. There wasn't a single speck of light except for what was shining in from under the crack of the door. I couldn't see him at all, so I had to rely on my other senses. His manly, clean smell filled my nostrils while his hands caressed my skin. I could only hear his soft groans and his heavy breathing that matched mine. Every touch was heightened and everything was so fucking addicting.

Daddy's hand slipped between my thighs. My legs were bare because he'd ripped my green-and-red tights in the office. One of his thick fingers trailed along my pussy over my wet lacy thong, stroking and teasing as I writhed against the wall. My thong was barely holding on since I hadn't had time to clean our drying come that had mixed together in a way that I really liked.

He added another finger and started circling my clit, making me bite my lip to keep from moaning. His free hand came around my neck, holding me in place.

I was at his mercy, for both my breath and my pleasure.

And I really fucking liked it.

My hands went to hold onto his forearm, and I bit down on my lip to keep myself quiet. I knew I was in no danger with Daddy. He promised he would take care of me.

"I'm going to fuck you hard and fast, do you understand? I'm not going to stop until I've painted your pretty little pussy with my cum. And you're going to let it drip down your legs and wear it for the rest of the day."

A shiver ran down my spine and my eyes closed.

"Oh, baby. You liked that, didn't you?" He whispered roughly in my ear. "You like hearing how I'm going to claim you for everyone to know, just like that hickey you gave me proves I'm yours." He's right.

I fucking loved that he was claiming me, even if it was just between us for now. I will know it every time I take a step and feel his creamy come on my thighs for the rest of the day.

I nodded furiously under his hand and I felt a gush slip from my pussy.

Daddy stepped back, pulling away just enough to free his cock before he thrust into me in one motion. Crying out, a hand is quickly clamped over my mouth.

"We can't have anyone seeing my baby as she's getting fucked, can we? I'd have to kill the motherfucker who saw you. Only I get to see you like this. Feel you like this." His words were punctuated with a hard thrust that made me see stars in the darkness.

"Only me, do you understand?" He growled quietly. I nodded. He didn't move his hand from my mouth and instead he fucked me faster. "Don't make a sound, baby. This is going to be very fast."

My eyes fluttered closed in ecstasy as I held on. Daddy would take care of me.

Thrust for thrust, breath for breath, touch for touch, we came together in a fiery display of passion that couldn't be more desperate. Two people needing each other so badly they fucked in a closet with minutes to spare until someone came looking for them.

"I can feel you holding back, my naughty little elf." Daddy whispered in my ear. "Let go. Give it to me, so I can come for you." His hand went to my clit, rubbing me quickly while fucking into me at just the right angle. "Let me fucking have it."

His words and his touch make me detonate, and I did my best to keep quiet, but let's just say that if his hand wasn't on my mouth I'd have alerted everyone. My pussy clenched down on his cock as I rode out my orgasm, chasing the release.

"Fuck, yes," Daddy groaned in my ear. His hips quickened and stuttered as I felt his come fill me to the brim. Again.

When he was finished we stayed locked together in the darkness, holding each other possessively and our breaths mixing as we calmed down.

"We have to get out there." I said, wanting to stay right here instead of going to work. "I need to go clean up."

His hand traveled to my throat again.

"Don't you fucking dare. I want my come dripping out of you, all day. So you know you're *mine*."

SIX

Seth

Someone was bound to out me if I took her to any of my favorite restaurants, so dining in was the only plausible choice to take her on an actual date. I placed the delivery order, and swept my eyes over my penthouse. I had the housekeeper come this morning and clean every inch. Offered her a nice bonus for her efforts, too.

This was the first time I'd had a woman over. Ever. I speared my fingers through the top of my hair. This restlessness was very unlike me.

My cell phone vibrated in my pocket and I fished it out.

Your place is on the highest floor? Why would you do that to yourself?

My lips twitched with a small smile. I could see her scrunched nose in my head.

She arrived faster than I'd anticipated. My wide stride ate up the steps to the door and I swung it open to see her beautiful face. She wasn't in her little elf outfit tonight. Instead, she wore a tight black dress with lace fabric at the hem. I didn't know much of anything about women's clothing, but it made her look fucking phenomenal.

"Hi," she chirped, grinning up at me as I swept her into my arms.

Her gingerbread and peppermint scent enveloped me. I groaned into her hair.

She wiggled in my arms and slid them around my waist. "I missed you too, Daddy."

My cock twitched against her belly. Every time she said it, I had a visceral reaction. She wiggled free of my hold and slipped under my arm to inspect my home

"Whoa, this place is huge."

I shut the door and went to her, wrapping my arms around her front and pressing into her back. She sank into my touch. My sweet girl . . . I grazed my nose against the top of her head.

"You didn't have to order me a car. Or pay for it," she mumbled and I just shrugged

It was my personal driver, but I didn't correct her. "So you make big bucks being Santa Clause every year?"

I chuckled.

"Most of this comes from the family business." She didn't ask any more questions. That was . . . odd. Without fail, women always asked more.

"Nice," she turned in my arms. Her blue eyes seemed to shine with how clear they were.

"Oh my, is Santa *excited* to see me?" She smirked, arching her spine to press into my hardened shaft.

"Naughty little elf," I said gruffly.

"Oh," she gasped, her eyes widening with understanding. "I believe you're mistaken, Santa. I'm on the nice list."

"Now you're lying?" I clicked my tongue. "You have to be punished." I banded my arms around her and lifted her up. Her feet kicked as she laughed breathlessly and her little movements rubbed against my cock.

She knew what she was doing to me. *Minx.* I set her on the table.

"Wait—" She squealed and I yanked her dress up over her waist. Her red thong had no embellishments. Sexy and simple. I curved my finger into the strap and yanked it. The cotton ripped easily, pulling a gasp from her pretty mouth.

"Mm, it's time for my feast." I grasped her knees and forced her thighs open, baring her cunt to me. Her creamy thighs lead down to her bare pink pussy and my mouth watered.

"Daddy," she cried, breathlessly.

I grinned at her. She watched me with her elbows propped on the table. Her chest pumped up and down as she watched me and her eyes held a feverish lust that called to mine.

Bending to reach her damp heat, I blew on her. She jerked as if I'd touched her. Her legs twitched against my palms. I grazed my nose against the start of her slit and growled. Such a fucking treat of a woman.

"Daddy," she moaned.

Fuck. I couldn't hold back anymore.

I ran my tongue down her slit, shallowly pumping my tongue inside her sex.

Fuck, she smelled amazing.

I ran my tongue up to the bundle of nerves at the top of her pussyslit. She whimpered and her fingers slipped into my hair, dragging me tight to her flesh as she arched her hips to relieve the desperate ache. I smiled. Her sweet nectar coated my tongue. I wanted more from her. I *needed* more.

Licking, teasing, and nipping, I rubbed my mouth all over her sweet cunt. She writhed on the table, her head thrashing back and forth. Her thighs continued to tense around my head. She was so fucking close.

The doorbell rang. The food delivery could fucking wait.

"The door," she gasped, pushing up onto her elbows.

I sucked on her clit and she screamed, dropping flat on her back. I slid my finger into her as I continued to suck on her clit. Her pussy clasped my finger, wringing it like she would have my cock as she came. Her bud twitched on my tongue, but I gave her no respite as she thrashed. Pumping my finger in and out roughly sent her over the edge for the second time.

Her legs lost all strength, and they continued to tremble.

Her chest rose and fell with pants. I stood, my hard cock aching in my slacks. I couldn't wait to slide into her tight cunt. To slide home.

But her comfort came before mine.

I strode to the side of the table and scooped her into my arms as her dress pooled around her waist.

"Let's get you fed and then I want you to come on my tongue again."

SEVEN

Julia

H is bed was fucking superb.

In all honesty, I was going to have to ask him where he got it because I knew I was never going to sleep well again unless it was on whatever kind of bed Daddy had.

Let's be real, I didn't know if I was ever going to sleep well again, unless I was wrapped up in his arms. That was all I wanted, to wake up with him wrapped around me, forever.

He was still deeply asleep, his warm breath tickling my ear as my hair fluttered over my bare skin. Every inch of him was touching every inch of me and I pushed my ass against his morning wood. Daddy rewarded me with a sleepy, throaty groan but didn't fully wake.

Ding, ding, ding. His phone started lighting up with a new notification. I did my best to ignore it, I wasn't going to go through his phone (how crazy would that be of me?) but fuck, his phone would not stop going off. *Ding, ding, ding, ding. Ding, ding, fucking ding.*

I finally reached over and grabbed it, just to silence it so hopefully he could sleep more. But when I flipped the phone over, his notifications all popped up. The sheer number of emails he received was overwhelming. 80 and climbing. But what caught my eye was the email address they were all being sent to.

ceo.seth.westin@westinmalls.com

What. The. Everloving. Fuck.

Seth, my Daddy, was the CEO of Westin Malls? My employer?

And he never said a thing? Not one goddamn thing? My heart raced and my breath quickened. I kept myself from hyperventilating, but my stomach threatened to turn.

I threw the blanket off me, desperate to get away from him. Was I just a joke? Embarrassment flooded my body, immobilizing me. So I really was just an easy fuck. Tears lined my eyes as despair literally broke my heart and threatened to rip my heart from my chest. I wanted to scream, to cry, to wail with pain.

Seth breathed in quickly through his nose, his eyes were heavily hooded as he looked at me through slits like he was still trying to wake up.

"What's wrong?" He said groggily, rubbing his eyes.

"Who are you?"

"What?" His eyes widened faster than they should have and I fucking knew.

"Who. Are. You? Really? You're not Seth Alexander, are you?

Seth sat up in the bed abruptly, wide awake with his lightly gray hair askew. "I am, I am Seth Alexander."

"You're not *just* Seth Alexander, though." I bent over and started to get dressed. "I need to get out of here."

"Wait, Julia," He sounded desperate and I knew I was right.

"No!" I screamed. With my dress half on, I turned to face him. All my emotions were clearly written on my face. "You don't get to ask me to wait for you to make up some bullshit excuse as to why you've been lying to me! Mr. CEO Seth Westin. What a joke I am." I sob-laughed and pulled my dress down. I went to slip my shoes on, but was met with a bare muscular wall.

"Don't go, please, let me explain." He was standing with his back against the bedroom door, blocking me. "Let me explain."

"Get out of my way."

"No, you have to listen to me. Please, baby." He looked so sad, so heartbroken that I almost did. But then I remembered how he's been using me, probably laughing at how easy I was for him. And it hit me completely. He felt no actual feelings for me, I was *just* a game. And I think that was what hurt most of all.

"Do *not* call me that." I poked his bare chest with my finger. "You used me. You lied to me. You made me think you actually cared about me but I was just a game to you. A pathetic little girl with a Daddy kink that you exploited. You're a cruel man, Seth *Alexander* Westin. And I don't want to see you again." I shoved him out of the way and raced out of the apartment, tears falling down my cheeks and my heart breaking the whole way back home.

One Week Later

The Uber I took from the airport raced through my sleepy little town in Michigan on the way to my parents house. I'd finally saved enough money for a ticket home for Christmas, just in time for a major snowstorm that left the whole town buried under white powdery snow.

A white Christmas, just like I wanted so badly.

It was exactly what I had wished for, but my heart hurt so much I couldn't breath. I couldn't do anything without the intense pain that had taken over my soul.

The snow made me think of Seth. Thinking of Seth made me think about what he did, and how angry I still was at him. Thinking about how angry I was at him made me sad and caused the heartbreak to deepen more.

"Almost there," the driver said, turning down the Christmas music that played over the radio. "You're just in time for Christmas."

"I'm here to surprise my parents for the holiday." I said, detached. Smiling hurt.

Making small talk hurt. I just wanted to get home and fall into my mothers arms and cry.

"That's very kind of you, I'm sure they're going to be over the moon."

"I hope so." I turned back to look out the window, hoping he wouldn't talk to me again and just let me fall into my sadness.

"Julia!" My mother came running out of the screen door as the car came up the long driveway. "My baby is home!" She cried happily. My mother was gorgeous, tall and willowy, her hair graying nicely and in a way I hoped I would someday. She smiled brightly at me, but when I tried to smile back, I knew it didn't reach my eyes.

And her smile dropped.

"What happened?" She asked.

"Nothing." I said, forcing myself to smile brighter even though I felt tears well in my eyes. "Everything." I muttered, dropping my bag and collapsing into the safety of my mother.

"Oh honey," She patted my back lovingly. "Do you love him?"

I cried harder, sobbing against her shoulder. "I think I do."

"Come in, let's talk about it." My mother guided me inside, and I was hit with the sense of home as soon as I walked through the door.

I might have been falling apart, but at least I was with people who loved me.

––––––––

Buzz, buzz.

Buzz, buzz.

Buzz, buzz.

"He's really trying to get in contact with you." My dad nodded his head, gesturing towards my phone that wouldn't stop buzzing with notifications.

"Yeah, he is." I shrugged, putting a card down for our game of crazy eights.

"Have you read any of them?"

"Nope." I said, popping the p and drew another card.

"I don't blame you. Let the bastard suffer." He smiled, supportive as ever. "When do you have to go back?"

"Two days. School starts back up soon and

I can't miss any days. Plus I have to find a new job now that the holidays are over." Well, that and because I refused to work for him.

"You'll be okay, you know that right?" My father looked at me earnestly, and I saw the pride he has in me, but also the sympathy. He knew how much pain I was in and he wanted to help, but also knew I could handle healing.

Buzz, buzz.

Buzz, buzz.

Buzz, buzz.

"Want me to tell him to fuck off?"

"No." I said softly with a sad smile, reorganizing my cards.

No, because what I really wanted was to see what he said. If he felt bad at all. But I didn't think I could bare to hear his voice.

EIGHT

Seth

E ven my office felt empty without her. I leaned against my desk, unable to stay still. The anxiety of everything that had happened made me crazy. I needed to move, I needed to take action. I needed to do *something*, anything to get her back. To get her to listen. I'd been up and down all fucking week. Since the last time I saw her.

She figured out my identity and now she wouldn't fucking speak to me. She'd disappeared and I was going crazy.

I'd gone through her personal file to get her address, and showed up at her apartment, but sitting out in the front had yielded no results. I'd even resorted to searching for her over the security cameras like a stalker but I didn't give a fuck. She'd left and I didn't even know where.

I should have told her who I was sooner. I knew I should have and yet, I still waited. I loved having her look at me without reservation. There was always one fucking way or another it went when women found out. When my last hook up found out, she poked holes in the fucking condom. Her knowing *me* . . . was an unmatched pleasure I didn't want to let go of.

All I could think about was her. I shouldn't have given her the day to think because as soon as I tried contacting her, she just . . . disappeared. Thoughts refused to let me rest. Was she okay? Where had she gone? Incessant, motherfucking thoughts.

I craved the little elf. I missed her. I'd been waiting for Rob to contact me about any information he could find, but he was taking his sweet time. I strode toward the door and pressed my palms against the door I'd fucked her against.

My cell phone vibrated. *Fucking finally.*

"What did you find out?" I barked.

"Chill, man. Goddamn."

"Robert Cade Westin, so help me god."

"Fine. Fine." He huffed. "She's in

Michigan, Lansing to be specific. Looks like she flew out about a week ago."

I stopped pacing. No wonder I couldn't fucking find her anywhere. I ran my hand through my hair.

What if she never returned to the city? What if she left me for good? I couldn't handle it. I wouldn't recover.

"You need to have a little more trust in women—"

I hung up to dial my secretary.

"Mr. Westin?"

"Book a flight for me."

"On it. Where to?"

"Lansing, Michigan. As soon as fucking possible."

NINE

Julia

I hadn't slept.

I'd barely eaten.

I knew that my parents were worried. I hadn't handled a break up like this before. Ever really. It truly felt like I couldn't breathe. Like each breath I forced myself to take hurt my body so much, I almost didn't want to take another.

I was so, so hurt. My trust in him was shattered. But I couldn't deny how much I *missed* his stupid freaking face. His arms around me. Feeling safe and loved at every turn.

I just wished that I could have had some closure. But I knew that that wouldn't really make much of a difference. I just needed time to fall out of love with him. My overwhelming love for him tore me down each day because I knew that he never felt that kind of love for me.

"Honey," my mother sat next to me on the window ledge where I looked out at the falling snow. It was so peaceful. So serene. So different from the sorrow I felt inside. I looked at her, suddenly feeling so guilty that I'd spent the time here with them moping around. "Can I get you anything?"

I shook my head no.

"I know you have to go back soon, but I'm worried."

I'm worried, too. I thought, but didn't tell her. There was no reason to make her worry any more than she already was.

"I'll be fine, Mom. I promise. It's just an embarrassing break-up."

"But you said you loved him."

"I did. I do." I sighed, wrapping my arms around my knees, tucking them to my chest.

"So, it's not 'just a break-up'." She put her hand on my back reassuringly. "It's okay to feel the heartbreak. It's okay to not know what you want exactly. All your father and I want is for you to be happy. To love and to be loved the way you deserve. That doesn't always come easy." She said kindly.

"What if he broke my trust? How are we supposed to come back from that?" A tear slipped down my cheek.

"Did he have a good reason for doing what he did?"

"I don't know." I answered honestly. "I didn't exactly give him the chance to explain."

"I think in order for you to either move on or to forgive him, you need to find out *why* he did what he did."

"Probably." I wiped my cheeks free of tears when we heard the *ding-dong* of the front door.

"Were you expecting someone?" I asked mom.

"Not in this weather." She got up and answered the door. When she opened the door, a wide smile cross her face. "I can guess who you are. Come in out of the snow. You'll catch a cold." She waved in the mystery guest, and as they rounded the corner, my jaw dropped.

Daddy.

Fuck, no. Seth.

I stood quickly, the blanket I had covering my lap fell to the ground.

"Seth."

"Julia." It was not fair how good he looked.

His cheeks were flushed from the cold, snow still melting in his salt-and-pepper hair as he stood in the foyer. His dark eyes looked at me with longing. Seth ran a hand through his hair and pulled his own hoodie down to straighten it out like he would a suit jacket. He shook his head when he realized what he had done, and moved both hands to hold onto the shoulder strap of his bag. His mouth opened and closed again quickly like he wanted to say something, but stopped himself.

"What are you doing here?" I walked closer, tugging at the sleeves of my oversized hoodie so they covered my hands.

"I had to see you," he said, running a hand through his hair. "I... Julia, I need to tell you, I want to tell you..." Daddy, dammit, *Seth*, never struggled with words.

"I think I'm going to let you guys chat." My mom awkwardly walked backwards out of the room, giving us privacy to have this discussion. Seth gave her an awkward nod and turned back to me.

"What?" Crossing my arms over my chest, I tipped my chin up to put on a facade that I wasn't as broken as I was.

As he'd made me.

"Julia, I'm so sorry. Fuck, I'm sorry." In a

few strides he crossed the room to stand before me, reaching out to try and hold my hands. At the last moment thought better of it. His hands dropped between us and he looked so pained. "I want to explain—please. Just give me 10 minutes of your time and if you still hate me, I'll accept it."

I looked out at the snow again and am thrown back into the memory of us in the fake snow he'd given me.

"Fine, 10 minutes." I shrugged and guided him the sitting room. I curled into the arm of the couch and made no move to invite him. He could figure it out for himself.

"Well, I'm Seth Westin. As you know." He slipped the backpack that was slung over his shoulder on the floor and followed me. He sat on the opposite side of the couch, staying a respectable distance apart.

"Obviously."

"Baby," he said, and I gave him a scathing look. "I'm sorry. Julia. I'm Seth Westin, CEO and owner of Westin Mall. Well, Westin Mall and a few other companies."

"Why didn't you tell me?"

He sighed heavily and scooted closer to me. "When you're as wealthy and as successful as I am, there are always people waiting to take advantage. Every single woman or man I've met within the last five years has only wanted me for one thing or another. My money. My name. My connections. They wanted what I could give them, but they never wanted *me*. When I saw you standing there that day, in that horrible little elf costume being harassed by that fucknut, I was instantly drawn to you. I had to know you. I had to have a moment of being just a guy who liked a girl. No games, no pressure, no worries." He looked so sad, so lonely. "I wasn't expecting you. I wasn't expecting this feisty, sexual, sweet, loving, *genuine* woman to be interested in me. I know the appeal I have on women, and with the chemistry we have, I knew being together would be the easiest thing I've ever done. The best decision I'd ever make. And it was. We were so fucking good together, Julia. Everything you craved, I craved. Everything you wanted, I wanted to give you. You are everything I want, everything I need." He had moved closer to me as he spoke, and the sincerity in his words made my heart ache.

"Then why did you lie to me? You knew me well enough to know I wouldn't try to take advantage of you!"

"Because I'm a coward," he snapped back at me, looking ashamed as he talked. Seth spoke again, quieter and softer this time, as I moved closer to him. "I'm a coward. I knew that too much time had passed and I didn't want you to behave differently." He scratched the shadow of a stubble on his chin. "I wanted to be the one to tell you, but instead, you saw the hundreds of emails I get every day for fires that I have to put out and meetings that I have to attend."

We stayed silent for a few moments while I processed everything.

"How can I trust you again?" I whispered and reached out to hold his hand. At the first touch of our hands, he held onto me like a lifeline.

"Julia, I swear to you, I will spend the rest of our lives making it up to you. I... I love you." He cupped my cheek and wiped a stray tear that had fallen. "I love you so fucking much and I want to take care of you, in every way, for the rest of our lives."

"You love me?" I repeated, making sure that I heard him correctly. He nodded with a smile and I bit my lip. "Good, because I love you, too."

Daddy pulled me close, resting his

forehead against mine. "I love you so much it hurts. You're mine and I'm yours. Forever."

"I like that."

He took my lips in a deep kiss.All my worries, all my fear, all my sadness melted away. When he pulled back, he breathed me in and held me tightly to him. Like he was afraid I'd change my mind.

"I'm yours?" I asked.

"You're mine. In each and every way."

"Daddy?" I whispered in his ear, mindful of my parents probably listening in.

"Yes, baby girl. Yes." He kissed me again, grabbing my hips so tightly it was almost painful, and I could feel just how far this kiss could go. How far I wanted this kiss to go.

I had to get us out of the house so Daddy could fuck me properly.

"Let's take a walk." I stood up quickly, taking his hand and dragging him toward the door, only stopping to bundle up and grab a few extra blankets.

Daddy didn't question it, just followed my lead and pulled on the thick jacket I'd offered him.

"We won't wait up!" My mom called out with a good-natured chuckle and I slammed the door shut behind me.

Seth

"Are you sure no one comes this way?" I pressed my palm against her spine, guiding her to the quiet, lonely structure a ways down from her family's home.

"Not really, it's my mom's old work office." Snow crunched under our boots as we neared the sturdy building.

Perfect. I pulled her inside the shack and shut the door. It was dark and dusty, but at least we wouldn't have an audience for what I *had* to do to her.

Whirling her around, I cupped her face and kissed her with everything that had built over the last week.

"Don't ever fucking disappear on me like that again," I said gruffly against her lips. The moonlight beamed through the window and cast across her eyes, causing them to glint. Her lips opened to say something, but I captured her mouth again. Licking and nipping them until she was a puddle against me. She moaned.

"I need you." I groaned against her mouth.

"Daddy," she whispered. I couldn't contain

myself anymore. I whirled her around and gripped the back of her hands, setting her palms on the wooden table to bend her over. That fucking hoodie was so long it covered her ass, so I was surprised to find the tiniest fucking shorts known to man under it.

Delving under her hoodie, I pushed it up and ripped those shorts down before I jerked her thong to the side, baring her smooth ass. I groaned, bowing my head forward against her neck, I reached an arm across her front and slipped a digit inside her. Her pussy sucked on my finger. She was ready for me. So fucking ready, so fucking wet.

I couldn't hold myself back any longer. I'd missed this woman. So fucking much. My little elf.

I jerked my slacks zipper down and my cock bobbed free with cum glinting on the tip. Taking her hips in my hands, I propped her higher so her chest was held up by the surface. The position lined us up perfectly. In a smooth glide, I slammed inside her and she took me with ease. Her wet channel clenched my shaft, as if telling him she missed him.

I groaned in ecstasy, my eyes sliding shut. The slap of my thighs smacking into her ass was an aphrodisiac in itself. Her moans and whimpers filled the small room, as we both thrust against each other to find our peaks.

I swore to god, the universe, all that was fucking holy, that I would fuck this pussy for as long as I lived.

One Year Later

JULIA

This past year had been the best year of my life.

The type of year I never thought I'd ever get to experience.

Now that everything was out in the open between Seth and I, that meant I got to know the *real* Seth. I always knew he was a Daddy, but damn, watching him bark orders over the phone, shirtless and pacing through the bedroom... He had suddenly become a *business Daddy* that was ruthless and powerful. Someone that wouldn't let me down. Someone that would take care of me no matter what.

Everything that had happened last year was hard, but it only made the two of us more grateful for each other. It made every day more special somehow because we knew how devastating it felt to be without the other.

Two weeks after we returned from my parents house in Michigan, Daddy asked me to move in with him. Aside from him wanting to simply live with me, he had said that he 'didn't want me working when I should be focused solely on school' and he 'knows how fucking irresistible I am so he doesn't want anyone at his mall looking at his girl.' And while I wanted to call him out for trying to possess me, another bigger part of me actually *really* liked it.

A month after we returned from Michigan, Daddy told me that he was going to marry me and that a formal proposal would be coming sooner rather than later. I understood that he was older than I was and so he wanted to get started on the next stage of our lives together, but I wanted to make sure that I finished school first. While Daddy said he got it, it didn't mean that he didn't bring up the subject every single time we had sex.

He'd be fucking me within an inch of my life and say how much better it would be if he could call me his little wife. He'd be pulling my hair and thrusting into me from behind and calling me his wife.

Every single time he mentioned it, I felt a shiver and I'd definitely get so much wetter. I knew it. He knew it.

I really liked him calling me his wife, maybe just as much as him calling me baby girl or naughty little elf.

So, there we were, back in *The Christmas Spot*, watching while some other elf and Santa made all the kids in line very happy. Ever since it closed for the season last year, Seth had been thinking about ways to make it even better. He said it held a special place in his heart and wanted it to be even bigger, even brighter, even more magical, than it was last year.

Fucking swoon. Everything out of that man's mouth made me swoon.

"You did a really good job," I nudged his shoulder as we stood, looking at the line of children and parents. We could only see smiles as far back as the line went. Seth had made sure to hire additional elves this year, along with a play center with present wrapping 'lessons', toy making demonstrations, freaking reindeer picture opportunities. Then off to the side, in the very back, was a snow pit. He had made sure to include a place where kids could make snow angels.

"I wanted to make sure that everyone had as magical of a Christmas as I had last year." Daddy held my hand, drawing me closer to his body.

"Well, I think you've succeeded."

"Come on, baby. Our dinner reservation is soon." He nodded to the head elf, the new manager who was 100% not a creep. " I have a whole evening planned."

"Let's go," I smiled brightly, trying to wait for the perfect moment to give him a gift of my own.

"I ate way too much." I groaned as we walked through the park, enjoying the fresh powdered snow fall that arrived as we ate. It truly was an amazing night. We got to sit in the coziest, nicest restaurant together, sipping coffee and eating delicious food, holding hands while we watched the snow fall to the ground making it a winter wonderland that we hadn't had last year.

Perfect.

"It was so worth it though." He chuckled, our fingers linked between us.

We walked for a bit, silently, and observed the beauty.

"This has been such a great year, baby." Seth broke the silence, stopping us right in front of an open snow-covered field surrounded by frost-covered trees.

"The best."

"I vow to you, to never take you for granted, to always be thankful that we found each other, to take care of you with everything I have, to protect you and to love you with everything I am. I never want to be without you, baby girl. Will you marry me?" Daddy slipped down on one knee and held up the most beautiful engagement ring I'd ever seen.

My mouth dropped open in shock, but the answer was immediate.

"Yes," I breathed.

His smile could have lit up the whole park. Daddy stood up and pulled me to him in a crushing kiss.

"Really?" he asked when we parted.

"Every day. For the rest of our lives." I whispered against his lips and pulled him down to kiss him again.

As our kisses got more heated, we became

more and more entangled. He pulled me into his arms but I lost my footing, tangling my legs with his, unbalancing both of us. We fell into the snow with a *thud*. Seth landed on top of me, his body draped over me, but I didn't feel any of his weight. Just his heat, warding off the cold of the ground.

"I have a surprise for you, too." I kissed his jawline, reaching down to pull the object from my jacket pocket.

"What could make this day more perfect?" He said, like there wouldn't be anything that could make him happier than me agreeing to become his wife.

Little did he know.

"I know you're my Daddy, but maybe you could also be my baby daddy?" I asked with a coy smile, holding up the black and white photo that showed the small baby growing safely in my belly.

Seth sat up, bringing me up with him and looked at the photo intently. Slowly, he looked at me with a smile that said he didn't know if he could be that lucky.

"Are you sure?"

"We're going to have a baby," I said with a grin, and gave him a kiss on his cheek. I moved to wrap my arms around him and straddle his lap in the snow. Daddy wrapped his arms around me, kissing me deeply with so much love I felt like I could burst.

A hand slid down to my belly where a small but very there bump was beginning to form.

"This is... This is the best Christmas ever."

Maya's Afterword

I feel so honored that you took the time to read My Secret CEO Santa. I hope you enjoyed Seth & Julia 🖤

I invite you to join my Facebook ARC & Street Team Group to get access to more announcements. There are so many books with daddy MMC's coming!

xoxo,
Maya Moore

Alina's Afterword

Thank you SO much for giving My Secret CEO Santa a read and coming with us on this journey. We hope you liked Seth and Julia's story! We really enjoyed writing it! Maya and I got on the phone one day, and after 15 minutes of chatting we had a good idea of these characters. The further we got into the story, the more they sprang off the page. Hopefully it was that perfect mix of holiday anticipation and nostalgia, and spicy Daddy smutty-goodness we all enjoy.

Happy Holidays, lovelies, and we will see you in the new year!

About Maya

As a lover of romance in all forms, Maya strives to bring spicy and satisfying stories to life. When she's not writing or hanging out with her dogs, it's highly likely she's in bed reading a good book.

About Alina

Alina Martyn is a writer of all things romance. Her dream has always been to write of fairy tales and love, and she does. Her stories are just much darker and spicier now. She gets to live out her dreams while also raising her three young children with her husband in the Midwest where she always tries to do better than the day before.